THE FIRST LADY

AN EROTIC ADVENTURE

VICTORIA RUSH

VOLUME 32

JADE'S EROTIC ADVENTURES - BOOK 32

COPYRIGHT

FEEL THE RUSH:

Jade's Erotic Adventures – Book 1

When lonely divorcée Jade seeks to broaden her horizons, she's invited to a private dinner event which promises to stimulate all of her senses. Wearing nothing but masquerade masks, dinner guests receive special service under the table while their fellow diners look on...

The Dinner Party

Jade's Erotic Adventures - Book 2

Jade discovers an exotic adventure club where strangers meet to explore each other's bodies in mysterious dark rooms. Using special effects to project swirling light patterns onto their figures, the shifting shadows provide just enough illumination to highlight their naked bodies while protecting their identities...

The Dark Room

Jade's Erotic Adventures - Book 3

Jade discovers a yoga club where members stretch and explore each other's bodies in the buff. She books an appointment, and during the first session meets a young redhead who tantalizes her with her flexibility and stunning body...

Naked Yoga

For the uninhibited...

SPICY ADVANCE EXCERPT:

I knelt down slowly until I reached her midsection, then I placed the bottom half of her dress over my head while I pulled her panties down to her ankles. Then I leaned forward, engulfing her inflamed clit in my mouth, running circles over the hard nub while I curled my fingers inside her pussy toward her sensitive G-spot. It didn't take long for Liz to begin moaning more loudly, and as her pleasure began to inexorably rise, she placed her hands over the back of my head, caressing me softly while my tongue danced over her burning gland.

After about sixty seconds of sustained stimulation on her bulb, she lifted her right leg and tilted her pelvis toward my chin, pressing her pussy harder into my face. I could feel the inside of her vagina beginning to tent and I knew she was nearing the precipice, so I sucked her button hard into my mouth while fluttering my fingers against her G-spot. Within seconds, she gasped as her whole body lurched forward in a series of spastic jerks as the walls of her pussy pulsed firmly against my embedded fingers.

I held her gently in my mouth until her contractions

stopped and her breathing began to return to normal, then I lifted myself up and kissed her gently on her lips. We heard the sound of another woman's shoes entering the room, and Liz lifted her finger to her lips signaling for me to be quiet while she peered through the crack in the door. Then she quickly pulled her panties back up and leaned in to whisper in my ear...

1

———

After a long day of schmoozing at my local political fundraiser, I dragged myself into the nearest Starbucks for a much needed break. I'd been invited to the event by the mayor's wife, and knowing that an election was just around the corner, I was eager to plant some seeds for potential work designing the team's campaign material. A commission helping to design their website and political banners would be a major feather in my cap and be a major stepping stone for networking with other bigwigs in the party apparatus. But after three straight hours of genuflecting and kissing ass, I needed some downtime to rest my brain and reclaim my soul.

After grabbing my almond-milk Americano at the pick-up counter, I ambled over to the one remaining seat in the corner of the shop, where an attractive woman sat alone nursing a warm beverage. It seemed odd to me that she was wearing a headscarf and sunglasses indoors, and although it was obvious that she wanted to be alone, I desperately needed to get off my feet.

"Do you mind if I take this last open chair?" I said,

motioning to the chair directly opposite her.

"No, of course," she said distractedly, lost in thought.

"I'm sorry to intrude," I said, kicking off my shoes under the table. "But I've been standing all day and my feet are killing me."

"I know the feeling," the woman said, smiling half-heartedly.

Her face looked vaguely familiar, but it was hard to place her under her heavy camouflage. She looked to be about my age, maybe just a few years older, with wavy brown hair and perfectly coiffed, arching eyebrows. With her soft flushed cheeks and clear lip gloss coating her full sensuous lips, she could have easily passed for a matinee idol.

But it was her unusual *outfit* that attracted my attention the most. Wearing an off-the-shoulder, tight-fitting black chiffon dress with flared sleeves and sparkling diamond hoop earrings dangling from her ears, she definitely didn't look the part of the average Starbucks customer.

"You look like you could use a little respite from the elements too," I said. "What brings you into our community coffee shop on this cold wintry day?"

"Just needed a break from all the hubbub, I guess. A few too many boring meetings."

"*Meetings*?" I said, glancing down at her curvy figure outlined by her clingy dress. "If you don't mind my saying, you don't look dressed for a typical business meeting. I gotta say, you're *rocking* that dress."

"Thanks. They're not your typical business meetings. There's a lot of high-powered people. I guess I'm expected to look the part."

I caught her glancing in the direction of an adjacent table where two stiff young men dressed in gray business suits wearing earpieces watched her intently. I jerked suddenly when I began to put the pieces together. High powered business meetings. An important political convention in town. A classy woman dressed to the nines accompanied by a security detail. I had the crazy fortune to be sitting next to the President's wife!

"Oh my God!" I gasped. "You're the–"

"*Shh!*" she whispered, lowering her head and turning her body toward the corner of the room. "It's hard enough trying to maintain a low profile with these goons following me everywhere I go. Can we try to keep this little secret between the two of us?"

"Of course," I said, pushing back in my seat in shock. "I didn't mean to... It's just–"

"No worries," the First Lady said. "No need to get overly excited. I'm just another commoner in our humble little republic."

"I'd hardly call you that," I chuckled. "Even without all the trappings of political office, you're a long way from *common.*"

"Thank you," she said, blushing slightly.

"Are you here for the Democratic fundraiser?" I asked. "I didn't see you at the convention center today."

"I try to leave all that political glad-handing to the big boys," she said. "I put in an appearance every now and then to demonstrate that all is happy and well with the first family and so the president can show off his eye candy, but otherwise I try to stay out of the affairs of the state as much as I can."

I peered at the First Lady through squinted eyes and nodded. It must have been tiring following her husband all around the country to various official functions, having to put on her game-face all the time. But there was something in her slack jaw and sad eyes that suggested there was a little more at work than just the harried life of a high-ranking political wife.

"I can appreciate that," I nodded. "Having spent enough time around all these politicos myself, I understand how exhausting it can be."

"What's *your* connection to the fundraiser, if I can ask?"

"I'm a freelance graphic designer. It's mostly a bunch of networking. There's a lot of money flung around these political campaigns. Just trying to get my small piece of the pie, I guess."

"These things tend to be pretty closed-door affairs," she said. "Do you mind my asking how you scored an invitation?"

"I know the mayor's wife in a roundabout way," I said, reflecting back on our little dalliance in the wine cellar of billionaire Steve Bannon's estate at last year's Halloween costume party.

"Haley's a doll," the First Lady nodded. "How do you know her exactly?"

"We're just casual friends," I fibbed. "I think she was just throwing me a bone as a favor, to be honest."

"Mm–hmm," she nodded, pinching her eyebrows together suspiciously. "What kind of design work do you do? Maybe I can throw you little bone, too."

"Oh, ah–" I stammered, momentarily taken aback by her generous offer. "Mostly website design, banners, logos, that sort of thing. It's kind of boring actually..."

"Are you kidding me?" the First Lady said. "Online fundraising has long since eclipsed the traditional form of fundraising by a large margin. I wouldn't sell yourself short. My husband needs to take advantage of every little edge he can find. Do you have any samples you can show me of your work?"

"Sure," I said, tapping my phone to pull up my photo portfolio and turning it around for the First Lady to see. "These are some of the corporate commissions I've worked on. There's no government applications to speak of, but some of my logo and signage work could be easily adapted for political purposes."

The First Lady took my phone out of my hand and began swiping her finger across the screen, nodding her head as she scrolled through my portfolio.

"These are actually pretty good," she said, pursing her lips in appreciation. "I think my husband's tired old campaign team could use some fresh ideas like these. Do you have a card I can pass along to our national campaign manager?"

"Wow, um–thank you," I stammered. "That's very generous of you."

"From the looks of some of these *other* pictures in your library, it appears that you know Haley a little more than just casually. Are these photos from Steve Bannon's infamous annual Halloween Ball?"

"Yes," I said, wrinkling my forehead at the thought of her viewing my personal pictures. "I got an invitation through a friend of a friend–"

Suddenly the First Lady's eyes flung open as she continued swiping through my photo library.

"Is this *you* wearing that provocative cowboy costume? You were really letting it all hang out at the costume party!"

I reached out and retrieved my phone, blushing a deep shade of crimson when I saw that she'd seen me dressed up in full regalia with my faux cock and balls dangling between my open leather chaps in the Lone Ranger costume.

"Bannon's invitation encouraged the guests to be creative and wear as little or as much as we desired. I guess I wanted to make a statement around all those self-absorbed high-rollers and show them that men aren't the *only* ones who can swing a big dick around."

"Humphh!" the First Lady coughed into her coffee, spilling some of it onto the table as she held out her hand to her security team to signal that she was okay.

"I like your style, young lady," she said, wiping up the table with a small serviette. "I think you're exactly the kind of free-thinking woman my husband needs on his starchy old campaign team. What's your name?"

"Jade," I said handing her my business card. "Jade Jackson. I'm not exactly sure how I should address you. Shall I address you as Madame First Lady?"

"*God*, no. Technically, I'm a private citizen, just like you. The job of First Lady refers a role, not a public office. So there's no need for such silly honorifics. You can call me Liz."

"It's a pleasure to meet you, Madame–I mean, Liz," I said, holding out my hand.

"The pleasure's all mine," Liz said, clasping my hand warmly.

We held onto each other's hand for a long moment, and I felt a buzz of electricity course through me while I watched her pupils dilating in excitement as another part of my body throbbed in arousal.

"How would you like to attend a different kind of fundraiser, at the White House next week?" she asked.

"Who–*me*?" I said incredulously. "You're inviting me to the *White House*?"

"Yes," she said. "The President's hosting his annual Correspondent's Dinner next Saturday and I could introduce you to a few people in his inner circle who might be interested in your services. Of course, you'll have to dress a little more conservatively than you did at Mr. Bannon's party. A ball gown might be more appropriate in this case."

"I think I could manage that," I said, clearing my throat. "But how do I get in? I'm sure there's exceptional security..."

"I'll send you an invitation with a special entry code. Just show your credentials at the guard shack. I'll leave your name for them to usher you in. Do you think you'll be able to make it?"

"I'm think I might be able to clear my schedule," I joked. "Thank you for your kind invitation."

"You can bring a partner with you if you'd like. I'll likely be pretty distracted with official duties at the affair, so I don't know how much attention I'll be able to give you. Just enjoy yourself and try not to ruffle any feathers. If you present yourself well enough, I'm sure we can connect you with the right people to further your career."

"Thank you. I look forward to seeing you again."

"That makes two of us," the First Lady said, motioning for her security team as she stood up to leave. "I'm looking forward to having you join the team. See you next Saturday."

As the First Lady gathered her belongings and swooped out the front door of the coffee shop with her security detail in tow, I sat back down on my chair with wobbly legs. I could scarcely believe what had just happened. Not only had I met one of the most intriguing and powerful women in America, she'd invited me into the White House to meet the President and his inner circle. But there was something *more* than that. I sensed we'd developed a powerful bond in the short time we'd been together, and I sensed she felt it too. I slumped back in my chair breathing a huge sigh, wondering what was in store with this sexy, beautiful woman.

2

On the day of the President's ball, I flew to Washington, D.C. then checked into a hotel to prepare myself for the big event. I didn't want to get all rumpled and sweaty flying in my dress clothes aboard a packed commercial airliner. Besides, it would look pretty strange boarding an aircraft in a ball gown and high heels.

The only gown I still had in my wardrobe was a frumpy old prom dress from twenty years ago, so I definitely felt the need to upgrade for such an important occasion. I wasn't sure how extravagant I should be, but Liz had told me to dress conservatively, so in the end I chose a midnight blue satin gown with a long pleated skirt and a V-neck bodice that revealed just enough of my cleavage to show off my best assets.

Gathered at the waist with a round bump in the rear, it was suitably understated and sexy at the same time. To finish off the look, I bought some black Christian Louboutin four-inch pumps with his trademark red lacquer sole. I didn't know if anyone would be looking down that far at the gala, but if they did, I didn't want them thinking I was so destitute that I'd blown an entire year's clothing budget on this one ensemble (which I very nearly had).

At two p.m., I went to my pre-arranged appointment at the city's premiere hair salon, where I sat for two hours with a stylist who created a flat wave design that looked minimal but still contemporary and chic. When I climbed out of the chair, my hair shone with a radiance that reminded me of my teenage years swimming in the lakes of Northern Wisconsin, where the clear waters and natural sunlight created a soft, natural look. I had just enough time after my appointment to get back to my hotel and put myself together for the scheduled start of the reception at seven o'clock.

When my taxi pulled up beside the White House, I walked up to the guard shack where a uniformed officer checked my credentials. After confirming my name on the guest list, he unlocked a heavy wrought-iron gate leading to a stone pathway adjacent to the curved central driveway. Signs pointed the way to the reception area, where randomly spaced Secret Service agents made sure I didn't stray off the marked path. When I reached the tall colonnaded Front Portico of the White House, I ascended the front steps barely believing I was entering the home of the President.

After stepping into the main entrance hall, ushers directed me down a long hallway lined with pictures of past presidents into a ballroom the size of an olympic swimming pool. Lined with floor-to-ceiling palladian windows and three enormous crystal chandeliers, the room sparkled in the glow of the late autumn sunset. But what really attracted my attention was the guest list. Milling about the packed ballroom I caught glimpses of Beyonce, George Clooney, Leonardo DiCaprio, Scarlett Johansson, and many other celebrities. Scattered among the clustered groups were various members of the President's inner cabinet, including the Secretary of State and the Vice President. But nowhere to be found was the First Lady.

Feeling isolated and exposed among the high-powered group of guests, I headed over to the bar where I ordered a stiff cocktail to calm my nerves. After a few minutes, a handsome local news anchorman sauntered over next to me to make small talk and begin flirting with me. As relieved as I was to have someone to talk to, there was really only one person I was eager to see. Gazing out at the milling movie stars and celebrities while the newsman continued pestering me with his lame pick-up lines, I wished I had the courage to join some of the other important people in the room.

After my third drink, I noticed a flash of red emerging from the middle of the crowd, and Liz caught my eye as she began walking in my direction. Wearing a clingy off-the-shoulder, crimson-colored gown with a long sweeping train, she showed off all the exquisite curves of her voluptuous figure. With her hair pulled back in a pretty French braid, she dominated the scene as the most beautiful woman in the room. Which was saying a lot, given the glittering guest list.

When she approached the bar, she smiled at me, motioning for the bartender to refresh her spritzer.

"Jade!" she said, flashing her pearly-white teeth as she clasped my hand warmly between hers. "I was afraid you didn't make it. I've been looking for you all evening."

"Are you *kidding*? I wouldn't miss this for anything. But

I've been kind of hiding out here at the bar. I feel a little self-conscious mingling among all these famous people."

"There's no need to be shy," Liz said, glancing over at the hunky newsman still standing uncomfortably close to me. "Is this your date?"

"No," I grimaced. "I came alone. My preferences lean more in the feminine direction. But I felt self-conscious bringing a girlfriend with all the political implications and everything..."

"Nonsense!" Liz said, as my would-be paramour finally got the message and drifted off into the crowd. "Half the people in this room are gay or bisexual. Come on, let me introduce you to some interesting people."

She took my hand and led me to the other side of the room where I recognized some familiar political faces. She pulled me to the edge of one cluster and the group turned around to acknowledge her.

"Jade, this is Bill Holland, our national campaign manager. I've told him about some of the excellent work that you do and he was eager to meet you."

"Pleasure to meet you, Jade," Bill said, extending his hand. "The First Lady mentioned you've worked on some high-profile corporate digital campaigns. We could use some fresh ideas to extend our reach into the ever-growing millennial group."

"I think Liz–I mean the First Lady–might be overselling my portfolio a tad, but I'd be happy to talk with you about some of the programs I've managed and how we might be able to adapt them to meet your needs–"

"*There* you are!" a deep voice suddenly interrupted us as a tall distinguished man in a black tux joined the group. I looked up to see the President smiling at Liz, and he stepped next to us, clasping her hand tightly. "I wondered where you'd scurried off to. I feel naked without my beautiful wife by my side."

He looked more handsome close-up than he appeared on TV, and with his broad shoulders and imposing size, he certainly looked the part of Commander-in-Chief.

"You didn't look so lonely chatting up Scarlett Johansson and Jennifer Lawrence on the other side of the room a bit earlier," Liz said with a wry smile.

"Just trying to keep our guests entertained, dear. It never hurts to be seen in the company of some of the key media influencers–am I right, Bill?"

"Being seen with high-profile celebrities definitely adds to your star power, Mr. President," Bill nodded, kowtowing to his boss.

"Speaking of," the President said to Liz. "There's someone I wanted you to meet. Warren Buffet's been one of our biggest campaign contributors, and he's been talking about making a big donation to one of your causes. He's just over there on the other side of the room–"

Liz jerked the President's hand as he began to pull her away.

"I'd like to introduce you to a friend of mine, first," she said, turning toward me. "Jade Jackson will be joining our campaign team and I really think she can help take your online fundraising efforts to the next level."

"Pleased to meet you, Jade," the President said, shaking my hand politely. "I'll look forward to talking with Bill about how you might be able to help us. But right now, I've got some other important matters to attend to." He peered at his wife with a steely expression. "Liz, will you join me?"

As I watched the President and the First Lady walk away

from our group, I sensed a certain tension between the two of them, with Liz walking a half-step behind him with her arm outstretched as he pulled her along. She turned around and mouthed the words *see you later* to me, and I smiled and nodded passively toward her. I really didn't expect to see much of her again for the rest evening, except when the gala was over and the first couple bade farewell to their guests.

For the next five minutes or so, the campaign manager and I exchanged ideas on how to spruce up their online website, then he drifted away toward another group of heavy hitters. I was glad when the ushers announced that dinner was ready and began directing everyone into the adjacent State Dining Room. The room was filled with a collection of circular white-linen-covered tables festooned with gleaming crystal dinnerware and tall bouquets of fresh flowers. One of the ushers directed me toward a table half-way back from the Guest of Honor table with a small stage to the left, and he motioned for me to sit down in front of a tent card bearing my name.

I noticed the names of two other women in front of the adjacent chairs, and before long I was joined by the President's press secretary and the First Lady's chief of staff, straddling either side of me. They introduced themselves and made polite small talk while the rest of our table guests were seated, mostly comprising low-level press correspondents and administrative officials. The two women were both single and pretty, and I wondered if Liz had requested a last-minute seating adjustment after she'd heard I came without a date and that I had a sexual preference for women.

After the first course was served, the President stood to make a speech sprinkled with homilies praising the First Amendment while poking fun at some of his counterparts in the press. Then Jimmy Kimmel took the stage and launched into a monologue making good-natured jokes about the President and some of his more controversial political policies. It was all highly entertaining, and I enjoyed peering around the room at all the famous celebrities laughing and clapping along dutifully, but it was the First Lady who my attention was fixated on for most of the evening.

After Jimmy Kimmel finished his piece and the chairman of the correspondent's association took the stage to thank the attending newsmen and women for their journalistic integrity in a thinly veiled attempt to curry favor toward the incumbent President, I excused myself and asked to be pointed in the direction of the ladies' room. I didn't really need to use it, but all the political glad-handing was giving me an uneasy feeling in the pit of my stomach. I'd never been a strong proponent of any one political party, and all this genuflecting was making me rethink the whole idea of helping to push the President's agenda. Especially one who didn't seem to give his wife the proper respect and attention I felt she deserved.

After checking my makeup in the powder room mirror, I went into one of the cubicles and pulled out my phone, tapping on my favorite game of Candy Crush. I couldn't believe that I was attending the most coveted event in the most famous residence in Washington, and here I was sitting in a dingy cubicle playing a solitary video game. After a few minutes, I heard the clack-clack-clack of a woman's shoes entering the marble-floored restroom, and I peered under the door recognizing Liz's long red dress train.

I turned off my phone and held my breath while I listened to her attending to herself in the mirror, but it seemed to take an eternity for her to finish whatever she was doing. Feeling a bit self-conscious waiting for her to leave, I decided to flush the toilet and emerge from my hiding place to say hello. I didn't know when I'd have a chance to be this close to her again, and when she saw me emerge from the cubicle, she gave me a broad smile.

"Jade," she said. "I saw you head toward the washroom and when you didn't return, I grew worried about you. Are you enjoying the evening?"

"Yes," I lied. "It's fascinating watching all these beautiful people mingling, but to be honest I don't have much of a stomach for all this political maneuvering. I just needed to come in here and freshen up."

"I know exactly how you feel," Liz said. "Seeing all these rich and powerful people gushing over one another and self-congratulating themselves can get a bit tiring. You should try doing it twenty-four/seven, three hundred and sixty-five days a year."

"I can only imagine how difficult your job must be," I frowned. "You must feel like a prisoner sometimes locked up in this big fortress, having to play second fiddle to the most powerful man in the world."

Liz coughed, momentarily taken aback by my outspoken opinion.

"You seem to have a special insight on my unique predicament, Jade. Most people think I have one of the most glamorous jobs in America."

"I've been watching you most of the evening," I said. "It's not hard to see the signs of tension between you and the President."

"Is it *that* obvious?" Liz chuckled. "Have you at least been enjoying the company at your table? I hope Julie and Emma have been keeping you properly entertained."

"Yes, they've been lovely. But honestly, it's *you* that I

haven't been able to take my eyes off the whole evening. You look absolutely ravishing in that form-fitting dress."

"As do you," Liz said, taking a step closer to me. "That blue satin gown complements your eyes perfectly. You look sexy and elegant at the same time. You chose well. Bill has already complimented me on how smart and creative you are. I hope you won't let all of this political backslapping get in the way of your helping with the campaign."

"I'll be happy to do it as a favor for you," I said, feeling my pussy flutter the closer she got to me. "Anything to keep me working close to you–"

Suddenly, Liz stepped forward and planted her lips against mine, running her fingers through my hair as she plunged her tongue deep into my mouth. I gasped at the unexpected intrusion, but as we pressed our bodies together and ground our pelvises against one another, I flung my arms around her, running my hands down over the curvature of her ass. She pulled me toward one of the cubicles while we continued kissing, then she locked the door behind us and slammed me against the metal partition wall.

While we groped each other's bodies pulling on each other's dresses, I pushed her back against the other side and slowly pulled up the hem of her long red gown. When I finally managed to hike it up over her hips, I snaked my hand between her legs and felt her panties soaked as wet as a dishrag. Pulling them to the side, I thrust two fingers deep into her slit and she threw her head back against the wall, grunting in pleasure.

"Oh Jade," she sighed. "You have no idea how much I've been dreaming of this from the moment I saw you. I haven't felt like this in such a long time..."

"You mean *wet*, or the touch of another woman?" I

smiled, thrusting the palm of my hand firmly against her snatch.

"Wet, and *turned on*. James is such a passionless lover. The constant demands of his office have left me cold and dry for the longest time. You're the first woman I've been with this way."

"I'm glad we found each other," I said. "Because I haven't felt this turned on in a long time either."

"But you said you've been with other women–"

"Yes, but I haven't felt this strong a connection with anyone in a long, long time."

"Is it just because–"

"Like you said," I interrupted. "Being First Lady is a *role*, not a job. I like you for a million other reasons."

"We better do this quick then," she said, looking through the crack in the door. "Before my security detail begins to worry about me and checks up on me."

"Even in the White House washroom?!" I said.

"You have no idea how short a leash I have around here."

"Just lie back and enjoy it then," I smiled. "I want to make you feel pleasure you haven't experienced in a long time."

I knelt down slowly until I reached her midsection, then I placed the bottom half of her dress over my head while I pulled her panties down to her ankles. Then I leaned forward, engulfing her inflamed clit in my mouth, running circles over the hard nub while I curled my fingers inside her pussy toward her sensitive G-spot. It didn't take long for Liz to begin moaning more loudly, and as her pleasure began to inexorably rise, she placed her hands over the back of my head, caressing me softly while my tongue danced over her burning gland.

After about sixty seconds of sustained stimulation on her bulb, she lifted her right leg and tilted her pelvis toward my chin, pressing her pussy harder into my face. I could feel the inside of her vagina beginning to tent and I knew she was nearing the precipice, so I sucked her button hard into my mouth while fluttering my fingers against her G-spot. Within seconds, she gasped as her whole body lurched forward in a series of spastic jerks as the walls of her pussy pulsed firmly against my embedded fingers.

I held her gently in my mouth until her contractions stopped and her breathing began to return to normal, then I lifted myself up and kissed her gently on her lips. We heard the sound of another woman's shoes entering the room, and Liz lifted her finger to her lips signaling for me to be quiet while she peered through the crack in the door. Then she quickly pulled her panties back up and leaned in to whisper in my ear.

"It's one of my security guards," she said. "You'll have to wait in here while I pretend like I'm finishing up my business."

"Can I see you again?" I said, looking desperately into her eyes. I didn't want this little tryst to be the last time I saw her.

"I'll call you. Right now, I've got to get back to the function or the President will begin to worry and send his whole squad after me. Thank you Jade—you were even more magnificent than I imagined. Bye for now."

She gave me a little peck on the cheek, then opened the door partway and headed toward the sink to wash up. I peered through the crack and saw a pokerfaced woman with short cropped hair and a business suit nod toward her while she stepped back as Liz fixed her hair and makeup in the mirror. Then the two women exited the room as quickly as they had entered, leaving me alone and breathing heavily in my little cubicle. After they left, I tore off my panties and fingered myself to the quickest orgasm I'd had in ages while reliving the electric moment when I felt the First Lady's warm, pulsing flesh in my hands.

I didn't know when I'd see her again, but at this precise moment I felt like I'd lived a thousand years in the blink of an eye.

3

After the dinner finished and the guests began streaming out of the White House, I joined the long line where the President and First Lady thanked everyone for coming and bade them farewell. When it was my turn to face them, the President shook my hand politely and Liz winked at me, saying she was looking forward to working with me on her husband's campaign. When I got back to my hotel, I must have come a hundred times replaying the erotic scene from the White House powder room over and over again.

But the following morning, I woke up uneasily, wondering if the whole thing was just some bizarre fantasy. The President hadn't even remembered talking to me earlier in the evening, and his campaign manager had made no attempt to reconnect with me before leaving the building. Having not heard back from Liz and not knowing when or if she'd contact me again, I began to pack up my belongings to leave the hotel before check-out time. But just as I was about to close the door behind me, I heard the phone ring and I scurried back inside to pick it up.

"Hello?" I said breathlessly, pouncing on the bed.

"Jade?" a familiar voice said. "It's Liz. I wanted to call you before you left town. Did you enjoy the party last night?"

"Yes, of course," I said. "But it was all a bit of a blur, really. I felt a little out of my element around all those celebrities and high-powered political figures. Except when I was with *you* of course. I haven't been able to get you out of my mind ever since our little rendezvous in the restroom."

"Me too," Liz said. "I can't bear the idea of you returning home so soon. I was wondering if you'd like to meet up for lunch so we can continue our discussion about your helping with the campaign team."

"At the White House?" I said, wondering if she was going to invite me back into her inner sanctum.

"It would be better to meet you alone, where we won't be disturbed by the President's minders. Can I meet you at your hotel?"

"Of course," I said, feeling my pussy beginning to flutter at the thought of being alone with her again. "I'm staying at the Marriott Marquis, downtown. Would you like to meet in the lobby?"

"I'd rather see you privately, away from all the prying eyes of the press and the public. What room number are you staying in?"

"1402," I said, feeling my panties beginning to moisten, hoping we'd have a chance to pick up where we left off.

"Will two p.m. work for you?"

"I'd wait until the end of time to see you again," I said, elated to hear that she wanted to meet me again.

"I was hoping you'd say that," Liz said. "See you soon!"

After she hung up, I called downstairs to extend my check-out time, then I went back into the washroom to touch up my makeup. I wasn't sure if Liz had the same thing in mind that I did, but I wanted to make myself as irresistible as possible to maximize my chances.

The next three hours passed by agonizingly slow as I tried to pass the time catching up on my email and browsing through stories of the First Lady's public appearances and personal causes. When I read that her personal passion and primary cause was helping spread the word about the importance of animal rescues, I felt even closer to her. Not only was she drop-dead gorgeous with a body to die for, she also had a heart of gold.

Shortly after the appointed hour, I heard a soft tap on my hotel room door, and I peered out the peephole to see Liz looking back at me, glancing from side to side nervously. I opened the door and invited her in, then closed the door softly behind us. She melted into my arms immediately, and we pressed our bodies together, kissing passionately.

"You're going to smear all your lipstick," I said, pulling away momentarily. "What about lunch–"

"*Screw* lunch," she said. "I'm feeling hungry for something *else* right now. Besides, we won't have much time before my husband begins to wonder where I've gone..."

"Doesn't he have more important things to worry about?" I said, shaking my head.

"You'd think so," Liz frowned. "But he's always been overprotective of me and a bit jealous of other people stealing my attention. I suspect it has something to do with his incessant need to be in control."

"What about your Secret Service detail? Won't they suspect what we're up to if we stay in here too long?"

"They've learned to mind their own business and respect

my boundaries. Besides, my lead agent probably already knows we've got something going on after she walked in on us in the White House washroom last night."

"We better get *busy* then," I smiled, pulling Liz closer to my king-size bed.

"You have no idea all the ways I've been dreaming of making love to you since you left last night."

"Oh, I think I might have an idea or two," I said, pulling the bedspread down and throwing her onto the mattress. "I've been replaying this moment in my mind pretty steadily for at least the last twelve hours."

While the two of us groped and kissed each other awkwardly, we pulled on each other's clothes and undergarments until we were both naked on the cool hotel room sheets.

"Oh my God," I gasped, seeing her fully exposed for the first time. "You're even more beautiful than I imagined underneath that sexy ball gown. I've been undressing you with my eyes from the moment I saw you. I had no idea you'd be as exquisite as this."

Liz was tall and slender, with the tight, toned figure of a ballerina, her long legs seeming to go on forever. Her hips curved sexily around her bare mound, tapering to a narrow waistline, before flaring again to reveal perfectly shaped, full breasts that glistened in the bright morning light streaming through the sheer curtains of my hotel room. Devouring her like she was the last person on earth, I took her erect teats into my mouth and sucked on them voraciously while squeezing her firm tits between my hands.

"Jade," she panted, arching her back to lift her bosom toward my mouth. "God, how I've dreamed about feeling your lips on my skin again."

"My *fingers* weren't cutting it last night?" I teased, nibbling on her hard nipples with my teeth.

"Oh, they were *cutting* it, alright," she purred. "I liked the way you parted my folds and made me squeal like a little girl."

"You don't look so much like a little girl right *now*," I said, nibbling my way down her stomach while I caressed her firm mounds with my hands.

"*Hey*," she said, grabbing the sides of my head and pulling me back up toward her face. "It's my turn to return the favor. If *anyone's* going down on anybody in the little time we have together, it's gonna be me."

"Just how much time have we got?" I said, peering into her eyes with a wrinkled brow.

I'd hoped that her meeting me in the privacy of my hotel room would give us more time to explore each other than in the hurried and confined space of the White House restroom.

"I dunno, maybe a couple of hours—"

"That's plenty enough time for us to pleasure one another any *number* of ways. Why don't we try stimulating ourselves *together* before we start worrying about who's looking after whom?"

"I like the sound of that," Liz said, wrapping her legs around my ass while I moved up higher on her body, grinding my pelvis into hers as we kissed each other passionately.

With her hips tilted slightly upward, my bald pubis rubbed against her flaring clit, and she moaned into my mouth. I could feel her wet juices coating my mound as I ground my hard symphysis into her sopping slit while my own juices began pouring down the insides of her thighs.

"Oh God, Jade," Liz moaned. "You feel so good between my legs. Fuck me with that beautiful pussy of yours."

Up to this point, I would have been perfectly happy to bring her to orgasm without paying much attention to my own needs. But when she started talking dirty to me, I reached down and pulled her legs upward, pushing them far to the sides while I lifted myself up and squatted over her, mashing my dripping pussy onto her slippery slit.

"Holy shit!" Liz gasped. "*Fuck*, yes! Fuck my pussy with your hot cunny. You feel amazing–"

I leaned forward, kissing her passionately while we pressed our tits together, dancing our tongues in each other's mouths. While we rolled our hips against one another rubbing our nubs together, I arched my back and pressed my sex harder against her. I could hear the sound of our two voices moaning with increasing urgency as the sound of our wet pussies slapping together filled the room, and I wondered if her Secret Service agent was standing outside the door once again listening to all the noise we were making. But at this moment, that was the last thing I wanted to focus on as I reveled in the sights and sounds of this beautiful woman writhing and moaning underneath me.

As we rolled our slick lips together, I could feel Liz press her hips harder against mine while her grunting and breathing escalated in pitch and velocity. Suddenly, she dug her fingernails hard into my back and jerked her body in a series of spastic heaves as she moaned into my mouth.

"Yes, Jade!" she groaned. "I'm cumming, baby! Oh God– I'm cumming so hard in your hot, sweet pussy. Come with me!"

When she told me she was falling over the precipice, all the tension that had been building up inside me suddenly released like the floodgates of a dam, and I began gushing all over her flapping pussy as one powerful contraction after another began consuming me. I held her close while we pulsed against one another, fucking each other's mouths with our tongues.

It seemed to take forever for us to stop cumming together, but when the waves of pleasure finally subsided, I collapsed beside Liz and kissed her gently on her neck, breathing on her pinched nipples standing pertly atop her mounds like two alert sentries.

"Holy shit!" Liz panted. "I've never been made love to like that in my entire life."

"Because you've never been made love to by another *woman* before?" I said.

"No—because I've never been with anybody who exhibited that kind of passion before. It's like comparing a filet mignon with third-grade hamburger."

"I'm not sure the President would like to hear you referring to him as third-rate hamburger."

"Well, when it comes to lovemaking, I hate to say it, but that's kind of how I feel. Though he may have a number of other admirable qualities, he's never been terribly attentive or giving in the bedroom."

"Maybe he just feels the weight of the world on his shoulders..."

"Maybe," Liz said. "But I think it's a lot more than that. We just never seemed to develop that spark. I think he always viewed our union as more of a political expediency than a match made in heaven."

"So where does that leave us now?" I said, wondering how we'd ever be able to reconcile our rapidly growing attraction to one another with her continuing role as First Lady.

"Well, I don't know about you, but I'm in no hurry to end this. I can't imagine our going our separate ways, regardless of whatever working arrangement you set up with our campaign manager."

I peered at Liz with a pained expression, hoping to separate our professional relationship from our personal one.

"Isn't there some way we could find a way to work more closely together? At least close enough that we can find some more private time to be together like this?"

Liz paused for a moment while she considered the possibilities.

"There might be *one* way," she said as a sly smile formed on the outside corners of her lips. "Normally, the campaign team works out of their own headquarters on the other side of town. But I might be able to find a space for you to work in the East Wing if you'll be doing mostly solo design work on the website. I've already told the President we're friends. I think I can persuade him to carve out a space for you on my side of the executive wing if I beg and plead hard enough."

As excited as I was to hear her proposing to find me a permanent position at the White House, I couldn't help worrying about the implications of our involvement with her continuing relationship with her husband.

"I don't want you to overstep your bounds," I said. "I wouldn't want the President to suspect we've got something more serious going on than just a working relationship..."

"He's far too wrapped up trying to save the world and being the President of Everything to notice. Once I've got you installed in the White House, we'll have plenty more opportunities to carry on our little affair."

"Okay," I said, looking at her like a child who'd just had an ice cream cone pulled away from her. "But is that all you see this as—an *affair*?"

"Of course not. I didn't mean it that way. Right now, I can't imagine being separated from you for more than a millisecond. I haven't felt this way with someone in the longest time–perhaps *ever*. I see your job, as much as I honestly think you can help my husband's campaign, as really just a cover to keep us together. Let's take this one day at a time and see how it plays out. Once my husband is out of public office, we'll have more opportunities to explore taking our relationship to the next level."

I shook my head, realizing the irony of my helping to get him re-elected, knowing full well it would just make the hiding of our relationship all the more difficult.

"Okay, but I wouldn't want to drive a wedge between the two of you–"

"Don't worry about any of that right now," she mewed. "Let's just enjoy what we've created and savor the time we have together. Life's too short to worry about the pitfalls of following your heart."

Liz suddenly rolled on top of me, spreading my legs apart as she pressed her moist pussy against mine once again.

"But speaking of *wedges*," she grinned. "I wouldn't mind getting another piece of this before we have to separate for a little while..."

4

———————

The following morning, Liz invited me back to the White House, where she greeted me at the front portico then walked me down a long corridor, pointing out some of the areas of interest.

"To your right is the Kennedy Garden, which is a lovely place for an outdoor lunch when the weather is good."

I gazed out the tall windows lining the colonnade at the immaculately manicured garden with its pretty holly trees and colorful flower beds.

"And to the left," she said, opening a door to a large room with a giant screen and plush theater chairs, "is the Family Theater Room."

"Did you and the President ever consider having children?" I asked, peering into the cavernous space.

"We just never got around to it, I guess. With his busy schedule, we feared there wouldn't be enough time to give the kids, and he seemed far more interested in his political career than building a family.

"That's too bad," I said, peering down the long hallway with all its nooks and crannies. "This looks like the ultimate playground for young children, and with all the support staff at the White House, you'd have lots of help caring for your children."

"I suppose," Liz said. "But with the current strain on our marriage, I'm not so sure about our prospects for staying together. I'd never want to subject them to a messy public divorce..."

I looked at Liz with sad eyes, realizing how much she felt like a prisoner in her own home. With all the eyes of the world focused on her and her husband, it must have been extraordinarily difficult for her to keep up appearances when she felt so unhappy.

When we reached the end of the corridor, we entered another large building and turned right down another long hallway.

"This is the East Wing," she said. "Which officially houses my office."

"This looks like a pretty big building for *one* person's office," I said, peering up at the tall ceilings and imposing pictures on the wall.

"It also houses a few other functions like the office of the White House social secretary, the Calligraphy Office, and the correspondence staff. But fortunately for you, unlike the West Wing where the President and his staff work, there's a lot of unused space in this building."

Liz stopped near the end of the hall and turned to open an oak door leading into a large, brightly lit office.

"This is my office, with a nice view of the garden and the South Lawn. I keep the door open most of the time, and you're welcome to come visit me anytime you have any questions or you just want some company."

I looked at Liz with a raised eyebrow and smiled.

"Knowing the kind of trouble we seem to get into when

we're together, you might want to rethink that open-door policy..."

"You might be right about that," she said. "Fortunately, I'm about as far from the President during working hours as one can possibly be on this big estate, and he rarely comes down this way. So if you're feeling lonely any time, don't hesitate to barge in."

I peered around her office at the pretty paintings and the various artifacts arranged on her shelves. Prominently displayed on her desk and shelves were various photos of her and the President at various stages in his career. I picked up a wedding picture of the two of them on an adjacent shelf and smiled.

"You both look so handsome in this picture," I said.

"And *happy*," she said. "Those were our carefree days, before James started his political career."

"How old were you when you married?"

"Not long after college," she said, taking the picture from my hand and peering at it with sad eyes. "We met at Yale, where he was studying law at the time. I thought he was so dashing and handsome back then."

"He still *is*," I said, beginning to wonder if it was such a good idea for me to be working so close to her when she obviously still had feelings for her husband. "Where were you thinking of putting me up?"

"Oh," she said, putting the picture back on the shelf softly. "I almost forgot. I moved a few things around and put you in the office two rooms down. Come, let me show you."

Liz led me across the hall to a room on the other side of the building and opened the door, inviting me to step in. It was modest in size, but a large window streamed in bright sunshine, and the tall bookcases lining the walls made it look much larger than it was.

"It's not quite as big as my office," she said. "But you've got a nice view facing south and all the equipment you need to get you started on your project. I've left the login information for the computer on your desk. Bill has already sent you an email with some suggestions for updating the website. I've left his number in your Rolodex, so you can reach out with any questions at any time. Is there anything I can do for you before you get started?"

I looked around me at all the official trappings, feeling my heart beating a hundred miles an hour, suddenly feeling conflicted about my new role.

"Liz," I said, turning toward her with a furrowed expression. "I'm not so sure this is a good idea—"

"Shh," she said, placing her finger on my lips. "I'm sure this all seems overwhelming at this point. You'll have the support of my personal staff whenever you need anything—"

"No, it's not that," I said. "I could do this work just as easily from home, or from the campaign office for that matter. Are you sure—"

"Don't get cold feet on me now," Liz said, stepping forward to hug me gently. "I don't want you thinking you're getting in the way of James's and my marriage. It's been a marriage of convenience for a long time now. For all I know, he's carrying on an affair behind *my* back too. I want you here next to me. Give it a few weeks at least. If you don't feel as strongly about us being together as I do, I'll understand and we'll go our separate ways. But don't give up on this yet."

"Okay," I sighed. "I suppose it can't hurt to work on the campaign website for a little while, at least until we've revamped it according to the President's liking..."

"That's my girl," Liz said, raising my chin and kissing me sweetly on the lips. "Take your time easing into this. There's a kitchen at the other end of the hall where you can help yourself to coffee and snacks. Let's plan on having dinner together when you finish up today. I have some special plans for us later this evening."

After Liz returned to her office, I sat down at my computer and logged in, reading the long email from Bill Holland providing instructions on how he wanted the campaign website tweaked. Most of the suggestions made sense, and I tried to keep busy developing new design ideas for the next couple of hours. But I found myself becoming increasing distracted as the day went on, peering out the window at the large White House lawn with all the groundskeepers and Secret Service agents milling about. The more I thought about it, the more convinced I became that I'd gotten myself into a situation that could only end with someone hurt.

How could Liz and I hope to carry on our clandestine affair with all these staff and security people constantly milling about? Was our relationship destined to be another flash-in-the-pan, ignited by the undeniable passion we both felt for one another, but doomed to extinguish under the constant pressure and demands of her role as First Lady? What if our relationship *did* grow to become something deeper and more meaningful? How could she ever hope to extricate herself from the expectations of a watchful nation? America was just starting to acknowledge the idea of gay couples, but accepting a lesbian *ex-First Lady* was a whole other matter.

By the end of the day, I was having serious second thoughts about my continuing role in her life and thinking of heading home. But when Liz poked her head into my office around 4:30, she didn't give me a chance to tell her what I was thinking.

"Are you hungry?" she said. "The White House chef makes a mean stroganoff."

"I don't know Liz," I frowned, not quite ready to tell her I was thinking about leaving. "Maybe it's best I head back to the hotel..."

"At three hundred dollars a night? You'll go broke if you try living out of a hotel in this town. I insist. You simply *must* have a sit-down dinner at the White House at least once. Besides, there was so much more I wanted to show you–"

"Will the President be joining us?"

"He's got a late cabinet meeting that will keep him busy for another couple of hours. It'll just be the two of us. Come," she said, pulling me out of my chair. "Let me show you some more interesting parts of the White House."

For the next hour or so, Liz gave me a grand tour of the three floors of the grand residence, pointing out special points of interest such as the library and bowling alley on the ground floor, the beautifully appointed Red, Green, and Blue rooms on the State Floor, and the personal bedrooms and family dining room on the third floor. After showing me the master bedroom and personal living quarters on the top floor, she led me into the Yellow Oval Room, which led out onto the curved balcony of the South Portico overlooking the enormous South Lawn with its sparkling fountain and the Washington Monument rising majestically in the distance. The sun was setting to the west, and the white obelisk glistened with an orange hue in the fading dusk.

"It's magnificent," I said, looking at the picturesque setting with my mouth agape. "How could you ever grow tired of this view?"

"Well, you know what they say. Home is where the heart

is. I'm afraid there hasn't been much warmth in this home these past three years. But enough of the depressing news. Come—let me show you where you'll be staying tonight..."

"*What?*" I said, peering at Liz with a shocked expression. "You want me to spend the *night* here?"

"By the time we finish dinner, it'll be too late for you to find another place to stay. Besides, who hasn't wanted to spend a night in the famous Lincoln Bedroom?"

5
____

Liz grabbed my hand and led me back inside, where we turned into a large sitting room on the other side of the Yellow Room leading into a huge boudoir dominated by a large four-poster bed and a stone fireplace. Gold velvet curtains framed the two large picture windows, with tasteful Victorian-era chairs and settees placed around the foot of the bed.

"*This* is the Lincoln Bedroom?" I said with wide eyes. "It's even bigger than the *President's* bedroom!"

"Well, technically, they're the same size. Ours just has a bit more closet space. But yeah, it's pretty big, especially for one person."

Liz stepped toward me and kissed me hard on the mouth, thrusting her tongue inside my cavity.

"But we might be able to solve that problem with a little extra company."

Suddenly, I felt dizzy from the bombardment of my senses, and I went limp while she held me. As much as I'd wanted to run away from her only a short while ago, I was suddenly at her mercy, with all the same feelings and cravings circulating inside me.

"Liz," I tried to protest. "This is seriously too much. I don't deserve any of this."

"Nonsense," she said. "You've rekindled a passion and a joy for living that I haven't felt in ages. It's the *least* I can do to repay the favor. Besides, having you stay overnight gives us the perfect excuse to steal away when the mood strikes..."

She pushed me toward the bed and lay me down on the soft mattress, pushing my thighs apart with her knee as she looked at me with a devilish grin.

Suddenly, a loud ding sounded, and Liz turned around, frowning.

"That's the dinner bell. We better not keep our chef waiting. The staff's gone to a lot of trouble to prepare us a special meal, and we'll want to catch it while it's still hot. There'll be plenty of time for more play time later. Come—I'm famished!"

Liz led me to the northwest corner of the top floor to the family dining room, where the kitchen staff had prepared three place settings. The two of us sat down kitty-corner at the end of the table, where the staff proceeded to serve us a delicious three-course meal. By the time we'd finished, the sun had begun to set and I glanced out over the front lawn of the White House with its pretty, illuminated fountain. Just then, the President entered the room and peered at me with a surprised expression.

"I didn't know we were expecting *company* this evening," he said, obviously irritated.

"It's Jade's first day working on the campaign, dear," Liz said. "I set up a special office for her in the East Wing, and we were working a bit late. I thought I'd show her around and invite her to enjoy Pierre's specialty of the house. Since you were tied up in meetings and all..."

"Of course," the President said, pulling up a seat on the opposite side of the table next to Liz. "Is there anything left over for me? I didn't realize how hungry I was until I smelled the beef stroganoff."

"No trouble, Mr. President," the chef said, bringing another serving into the room and placing it in front of him with gloved hands. "And of course, we've saved an extra serving of your favorite dessert, crème brûlée."

"Thank you, Pierre," the President said. "You always know the best way to a man's heart."

"My pleasure, Mr. President," the chef said, backing into the adjacent kitchen.

"So how did you find your first day working in the White House?" the President said, peering at me as he took a mouthful of creamy pasta.

"It was all a bit overwhelming," I said, still hardly believing I was sitting down to have dinner with the President and the First Lady in their private dining room. "Liz has been such a gracious host and has provided me with *more* than I need."

The President looked at me suspiciously, then glanced over at Liz and smiled.

"How long have you known each other?" he said. "Liz said you were friends."

"Not that long actually," I blushed. "We met when you were attending the political convention in Chicago last week."

"You two seem to have formed an unusually strong bond in such a short period of time," he said. "Normally, Liz takes quite a while to warm up to new acquaintances. You must have made an especially powerful first impression."

"When Jade told me about the digital design work she's done," Liz interjected, "I thought it would be a perfect fit for our campaign. We just struck up a conversation and one thing led to another. We have a lot of the same interests and passions–animal rescue, AIDS research, gender equality..."

"It's good to have *passions*," the President said, nodding toward Liz. "I haven't seen the First Lady this animated about anything in a long time. Will you be staying with us long?"

"Actually, I've invited Jade to spend the *night*," Liz said. "She's a long way from home and I thought it would be fun for her to experience staying in the Lincoln Bedroom for one night. You know, something to tell her kids about someday..."

The President peered down at my right hand and cocked his head.

"Oh? Do you have children, Jade? I don't see a wedding ring."

"No, my first husband and I never got around to it. We split up long before the idea crossed our mind."

"So you're *single* then?" he said. "We've got lots of eligible young bachelors working in various administrative capacities in the West Wing. Perhaps you'd like to work on the *other* side of the executive campus where all the action happens–"

"I think Jade is perfectly happy with her *present* arrangements, dear," Liz interrupted. "It's getting late. I think I'll show Jade to her room and get her set up. Will you be coming up to bed soon?"

"I've got a late meeting with my chief of staff," the President said. "I'll join you in another hour or so."

Then he looked at me with a penetrating gaze.

"I hope you have a pleasant sleep, Jade. I'm looking forward to seeing some of your new work in the days ahead."

"Thank you, Mr. President," I smiled. "It will be my pleasure. I hope you like some of the new designs I've been working on."

"I'm sure I *will*," he said, stealing a quick glance down the top of my partially unbuttoned blouse.

After the President left to return to his office, Liz and I went back across the hall to prepare my room.

"That was kind of *scary*," I said to Liz when she closed the door behind us. "Do you think he has any suspicions what we've been up to?

"I think he's far too focused on his own self-important work to dream about any mischief going on behind his back."

Liz suddenly stepped forward, pushing me back down onto the mattress, then she climbed on top of me, spread-eagling her legs around my stomach. "But now that you mention it, there was one other dessert course I was looking forward to having before we turn in."

"Right *here and now*? In the *Lincoln Bedroom*?!"

"You wouldn't be the first guest to enjoy a little late-night tryst while sleeping over at the White House. It's kind of like being a member of the mile-high club. It's on every social climber's bucket list in this city."

"But I'm not a social climb–"

"I know," Liz said, beginning to unbutton my blouse. "That's just another thing I love about you. You don't have a selfish bone in your body. And you're not the least bit political. It's refreshing to have someone like you hanging around this ivory tower."

"Are you sure we've got enough *time*?" I said, peering nervously toward the closed door.

"He said he'd be gone at least an hour," Liz smiled. "That gives us plenty of time to enjoy a turn or two. Besides, there's something I've been dreaming about doing to you..."

Liz unbuttoned the rest of my blouse and removed my bra, then tore off her clothes, straddling one of my breasts while she rubbed her wet pussy over my erect nipple.

"Mmm," she purred. "There's *so* many ways to make love to your beautiful body."

"Oh yeah?" I grinned, suddenly forgetting all of my previous concerns and grabbing my breast between two hands, rubbing it sexily over her slippery vulva. "Do you like that? Do you like fucking my tits?"

"Yes, I do," she moaned, looking at me with a Cheshire Cat grin. "But do you know what I'd enjoy fucking even *more*? Your beautiful face, and those puffy rosebuds lips."

"Mmm," I said, pulling her hips higher up on me until they covered my face. "Sit on my face, Liz. I want to watch you writhe and moan while I eat your pussy."

"*Fuck*, yes," Liz groaned, lowering her dripping pussy onto my lips. "Suck my cunt like you enjoyed that crème brûlée."

"Mmm," I purred. "You're *much* more moist and tasty than the President's favorite dessert."

"Yes, she *is*, isn't she?" a deep baritone voice suddenly said from the other end of the Lincoln Bedroom.

We both jerked our heads to see the President standing in the open doorway with his hands on his hips.

"I *knew* you two had something more going on ever since you both ducked out in the middle of the Correspondent's Dinner."

"James," Liz said, bending over to cover up my exposed

body and pulling the sheets overtop the two of us. "I thought you had an important meeting?"

"What could be more important than watching my wife sit atop of a beautiful woman's face, moaning in delight?"

"You mean–you're not *angry*?"

"Are you *kidding* me?" he said. "I'm just thrilled that my wife has found a way to reignite her passion, even if it *is* with another woman. Besides, you know this is every man's fantasy..."

Liz peered at me under the covers, shaking her head in dismay.

"I'm sorry to put you in this predicament, Jade," she whispered. "I'll get dressed and get him out of here so you can have a little privacy."

"It's not a problem, really" I said, smiling at her under the covers. "It's not like I haven't been in this situation before. Why don't we make the most of it and have a little fun now that the opportunity presents itself?"

"Your mean–you don't mind playing it *both ways* sometimes?" she said.

"If the right man presents himself," I grinned, "I never pass up the opportunity to mix it up. And this man is certainly one in a million."

"What did you have in mind, exactly?" Liz asked.

"Why don't we give him a little show to start with? See if we can rev up his engines and rekindle some of that passion you say has been missing from your marriage all these years?"

"You're a *very* naughty girl," Liz said, giving me a huge smile.

"What do you say, dear?" the President said from the other side of the room. "Are you two going to have all the fun under the covers, or were you thinking of sharing in the spoils?"

Liz flew the sheets back toward the end of the bed and turned around to face her husband.

"Why don't you just sit down and *watch* for a little while?" she said. "I'd like to give you a little lesson in self-control for a change."

"Can I–um–at least *enjoy* myself while I watch?" the President said.

"No," Liz smiled. "I'd like to take a turn at being the Commander-in-Chief for a change. You're just going to have to sit there and squirm while the rest of the world revolves around *you* this time."

"If you *insist*," the President said, scrunching down in one of the old armchairs and spreading his legs with a huge bulge in his pants.

"What do you say, Jade?" Liz purred. "Shall we pick up where we left off?"

"By all means," I said, grasping the sides of her ass as she lowered her pussy back down onto my face.

But this time, Liz leaned forward over my head and rested her elbows on the pillows above me, giving her husband a wide-open view of her exposed ass and vulva grinding against my chin.

"Oh my God," the President groaned as he watched his wife roll her hips on my face and moan in delight.

"Does that turn you on, babe?" Liz said. "Do you like watching your wife getting eaten out by a beautiful woman?"

"*God* yes," he said, unzipping his fly.

"No *touching*, remember?" Liz said, grinding her snatch into my face as her juices began streaming down over my chin and my neck.

"I promise," he said. "I'm just freeing the beast. Otherwise, I might rip a hole in my pants from how hard you're making me right now."

"*Good*," Liz said. "Enjoy the show. Maybe you can pick up some pointers."

For the next two or three minutes, Liz proceeded to grind her pussy into my eager mouth while I danced my tongue over her clit and the President hummed and groaned in delicious torture from the other side of the room. For some reason, I didn't mind him seeing my exposed breasts exposed behind Liz's bare bottom–it just added to the eroticism of the moment. Before long, Liz began to shake her hips more vigorously against my face, and I sucked her clit deep into my mouth knowing she was getting close to reaching her climax.

When it finally hit her, she squealed out loud while I watched her tits bouncing and shaking above me in the throes of ecstasy. I cupped her ass tightly in my hands until I felt her buttocks stop shaking, then she lifted her leg and turned around to face the President. When we both looked in his direction, we saw that he'd pulled his pants all the way down to his ankles with his erection flapping up excitedly against his abdomen and a small stream of pre-cum dribbling down the underside toward his tight balls.

His cock was larger than most, perhaps eight inches long with a perfectly straight shaft and a large, glistening circumcised crown. He looked at the two of us with lust in his eyes, gripping the arms of the Victorian chair so tightly his knuckles were blue.

"My oh my, James," Liz teased. "I haven't seen you in such a state of excitement in years. Maybe we should invite an extra paramour into our bedroom more often. You look like you could pop off any second."

"It's taking every ounce of my strength not to pounce on

top of the two of you right now," he said. "This is torture watching you."

"Good," Liz scoffed. "Now you have a sense what it's been like being neglected all these years. I want you to see what it's like on the other side of the coin for a change. You just continue sitting there for a little longer while Jade and I have some more fun."

"Liz..." the President protested. "You can't leave me hanging like this–"

"Oh, I can, and I *will*. Just pretend you're sitting in the Situation Room with all your military advisors while you watch helplessly as the North Koreans taunt you with repeated missile launches over the North China sea. *I'm* the one in control, this time, dear."

"You're evil, you witch," he groaned.

"You have *no* idea," Liz smiled. "Jade, do you mind if I *watch* my husband suffer this time while we have some more fun?"

"Whatever you say, boss," I smiled. "I'm just enjoying watching you two build the sexual tension."

"May I remove the rest of your clothes?" she said, winking at me.

"We're in this pretty deep already," I smiled. "Knock your-self out."

Liz leaned over and unbuckled my belt then pulled my dress pants and panties down over my feet and threw them on the adjacent settee. Then she pressed my thighs upward in the same way I'd done with her earlier at the hotel, but this time she turned around and lowered her ass onto my pussy facing toward the President, in the reverse cowgirl position. With both of our legs splayed wide apart mere inches away from the President's ogling eyes, he could clearly see our dripping pussies touching and rubbing against one another.

Liz leaned forward slightly then arched her back as our engorged glands touched, and we both moaned in pleasure. I could hear the President groan also, and I could only imagine what kind of pain he was suffering not being able to join us or touch himself. As Liz began to slide her wet pussy over mine and moan in delight, she continued to taunt and torment her husband.

"Do you *like* seeing our wet pussies rubbing together, James?"

"God, yes," he grunted.

"Do you wish your cock was wedged between these two beautiful cunnies while we soaked you with our juices?"

"*Fuck*, yes," he groaned.

"Would you like to bury your big dick in my snatch while Jade's tribbing my hard clit?"

"Oh God, Liz," he whinnied. "You have no idea."

"I can see you dripping all the way down that big pole and over your beautiful balls," she said.

"*Please*, Liz," he pleaded. "Let me *touch* myself at least. You're killing me."

"I want this to be a lesson to you," she said. "About the power of a passionate, emotional connection. Like the one every husband and wife should share."

"Yes, Liz," the President nodded.

"Like the one every husband and wife should savor together..."

"Yes, baby," he panted.

"Do you want to watch me cum all over Jade's pretty pussy?"

"God, yes. Let it go, baby. Come for me while I watch your beautiful body shaking and quivering in ecstasy."

"Are you ready to cum with me, Jade?" Liz said, turning her head halfway around to peer at me.

"Damn straight, girl," I moaned, feeling my own climax barreling toward me like a freight train.

"Okay, Jade," Liz's voice squeaked, suddenly rising in volume. "I'm going to cum. Let me see you gush all over my twat. I'm cumming, baby!"

I grabbed the sides of Liz's ass and curled my pelvis up toward her hole, feeling the insides of my pussy beginning to throb and contract tightly. As Liz wailed at the top of her lungs in delirious ecstasy, I gushed hard jets of fluid against her pulsing vulva while my anus snapped open and shut mere inches away from her apoplectic husband. While the two of us bucked and screamed in orgasmic union, I could have sworn I heard the sound of slapping skin coming from the President's chair.

When Liz and I finally came down from our highs, Liz lifted herself off me and kissed each of my breasts before giving me a peck on the cheek. Then she lifted up both of our bras lying beside us on the bed and slowly ambled over to the President's chair.

"You've been a *very* bad boy, Mr. President," she said, noticing him holding his purple pecker in both of his hands tightly. "I told you no touching. I'm afraid we're going to have to take more drastic measures now."

As the President looked at her sheepishly, she pulled his hands off his dripping cock and forced them behind the back of his chair, tying them tightly to the backrest with the two bra straps. When he was sufficiently immobilized, she walked around in front of him and slapped her tits across his face, making them redden.

"You don't *look* like the most powerful man in the world

now," she teased. "How does it feel to be subjugated and controlled by the whims of a distracted partner?"

"Not so bad, actually," he smiled. "I could kind of get used to this."

"That's not what your *little* head seems to be saying," she said, noticing the streams of precum cascading down both sides of his engorged cock like a waterfall. "Don't you want to feel my warm, slippery pussy taking your big thumper inside me?"

"Yes, please Liz," he pleaded. "I want to feel you inside. I want to make love to you so bad right now."

"What do you think, Jade?" Liz said, smiling over at me. "Should I put him out of his misery, or are you enjoying this show too much?"

"Maybe just a little bit longer," I teased. "We don't want him to forget what it takes to please a woman and who's in charge now."

"You little–" the President started.

"*Uh, Uh!*" Liz shook her head, chiding him. "That's my new best friend you're talking about. From now on, *I'm* the one calling the shots as to what happens to her and what kind of role she's going to play in our campaign. Is that clear?"

"Yes, dear," the President groveled. "I'll do anything to reconnect with you. I just want to feel your beautiful, warm body next to me."

"That can be arranged," Liz said while circling around him, shimmying her ass mere inches away from the tip of his cock.

"Do you promise to love me, and hold me, and cherish me for the rest of our days?" she said.

"Yes, Liz. I've always loved you. I just never gave you the attention you deserved."

"Do you promise to tuck me in every night with a sweet bedtime kiss?"

"Yes, baby."

"And make love to me whenever either one of us feels the urge?"

"Oh *God* yes," the President panted, staring between Liz's legs at her glistening gap while she bent over him, tantalizing inches away from his throbbing crown.

"Even if North Korea or China have just declared war on the U.S.?"

"Um..."

"I'm *kidding*, you big brute," Liz said as she finally placed her dripping slit over his pulsing member and slowly slid herself down his shaft.

"Oh my God, Liz," the President groaned. "You've never felt so good..."

"Is that just because you're all turned on from watching me make love to Jade?"

"No, it's because I've never felt this close to you. Now I finally recognize how important you are to me. I'll never neglect you again."

"Okay, baby," Liz smiled. "I believe you. Now fuck me with that big President Johnson and let me feel you squirting inside me. I'm going to come again."

"Yes, Liz," the President groaned. "I'm going to come for you. I'm going to come like I've never come before in my whole life. Squeeze my cock while I come inside you."

While the President unleashed a howl of pleasure, Liz grabbed the two sides of the armrests and threw her head back in ecstasy while her pussy clamped down on the President's cock. I watched the two of them rocking and thrashing their hips together while the base of the President's dick pulsed in a series of powerful surges as he emptied his seed inside her.

I wasn't sure what my future would be in their administration, but there was one thing I was certain of at this moment. The President would no longer take his wife for granted again, and their bond would forever be unbreakable from this moment forward.

THE
DINNER
PARTY
AN EROTIC ADVENTURE

VICTORIA RUSH

Everybody's an exhibitionist in disguise

Spying on the neighbors just got a lot more interesting...

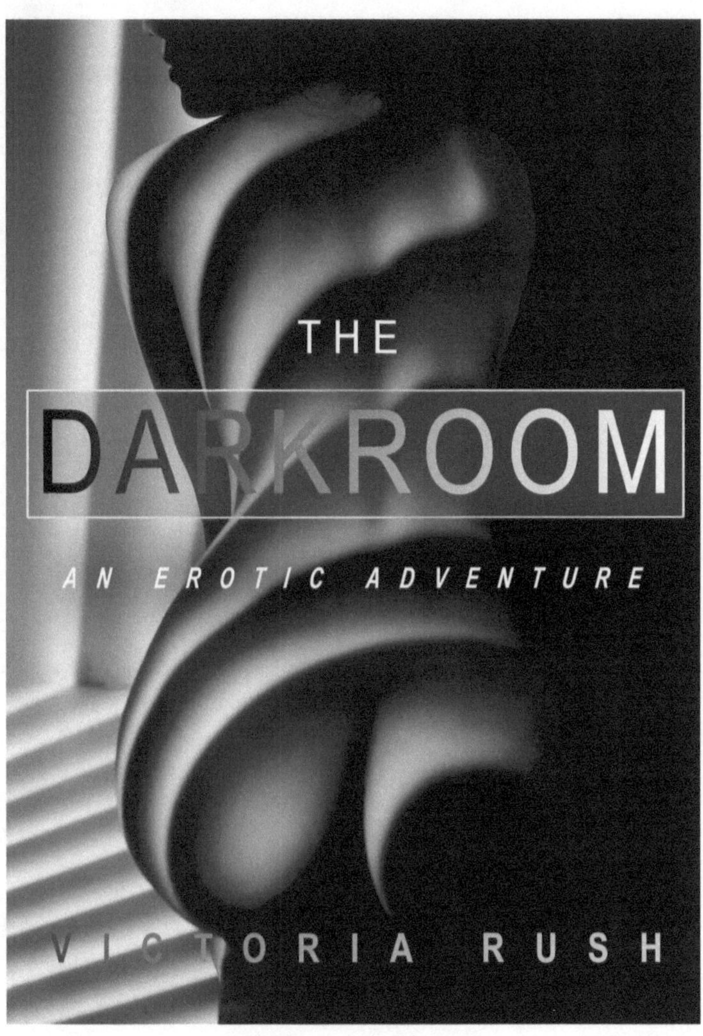

Everything's sexier in the dark...

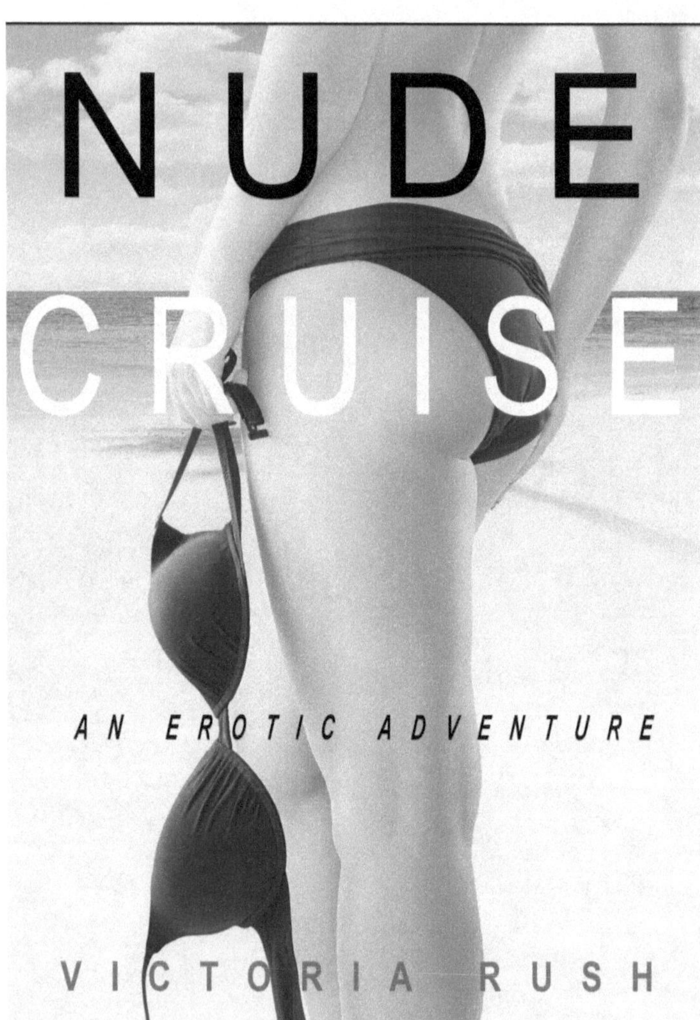

Some people get wet on a cruise for different reasons...

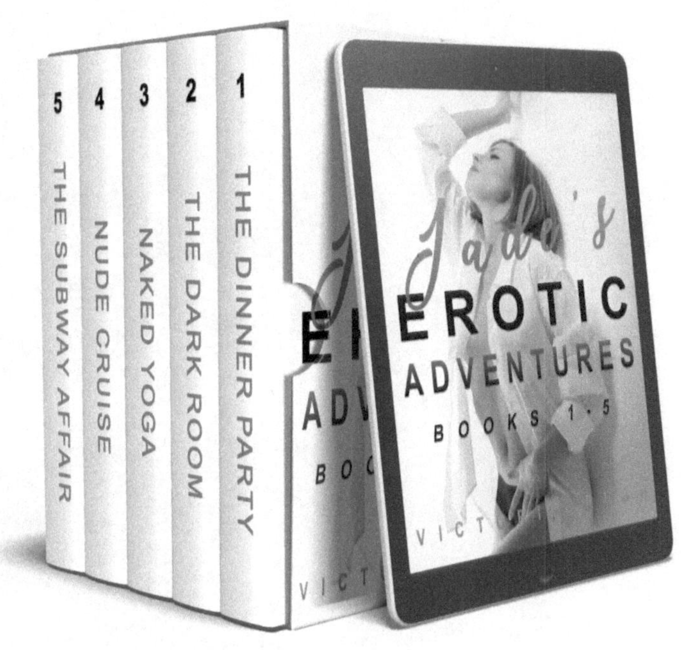

Books 1 -5 in the bestselling erotica series - 60% off

THE DARE - PREVIEW
CHAPTER 3

"Okay, so now that I'm committed, tell me where you had in mind for this little experiment."

"Actually," Hannah said, "I have a *series* of places in mind, each one more challenging than the one before."

"But I thought you said this was a one-off proposition?"

"I said nothing of the sort. I only said that if you won, I'd pay for the flights to Bora Bora. If you want me to cover the cost of hotels, food, and all the other incidentals, you'll have to pass progressively tougher tests. We don't want to make this *too* easy for you, do we?"

I crossed my arms and huffed, putting on my best pouty face.

"It hardly seems fair," I said. "But I'm still game. Besides, either one of us can pull out at any time to lock in our gains, right?"

"I suppose so," Hannah shrugged. "But what would be the fun in that? Something tells me once you've tried the first experiment, you won't want to stop. I think you're going to find this whole thing quite titillating and exciting. This will be the most fun either one of us has had in a long time."

I pushed the rest of my half-eaten salmon dish to the side, suddenly no longer interested in eating.

"Okay, lay it on me then. Where are you planning to take me for the first test?

Hannah gulped down the rest of her margarita then peered at me with a lopsided grin.

"Church. More specifically, a *Catholic* church. You haven't been in quite a while, have you? This will be your chance to repent and atone for all your sins."

"It's not like I've broken any commandments or anything–"

"The Catholic Church still considers sex outside of marriage a mortal sin. So technically, you've been doing a ton of sinning since your marriage ended."

"Well I haven't been a practicing Catholic for ages," I snorted. "So my conscience is clear. This'll be a cakewalk. All I have to do is sit quietly in my pew, right?"

"Yes, but it'll be a *front-row* pew, in full view of the priest who'll be delivering the sermon."

"Okay, but I'll be fully clothed, right? It's not like there'll be anything for him to see..."

"Not if you can keep your composure and don't cum all over the floor," Hannah said, cocking her head playfully.

"I don't think I'll have any difficulty keeping my dick in my pants, in a manner of speaking. But you raise a good point. You can't expect me not to get a little wet while you're stimulating me. What will I be allowed to wear?"

"I assume you'll dress appropriately, wearing your Sunday best. A mid-length skirt and button-up blouse should do the trick. You should be able to hide a few dribbles that way, right?"

"I suppose so, but how will we muffle the sound of the vibrator buzzing inside my panties? There's likely to be other people sitting around me in adjacent pews..."

"Never fear," Hannah smiled, reaching into her purse and pulling out a U-shaped silicone sex toy. "I've been talking with our friend at the local Babeland store. She's given me the latest prototype of the We-Vibe vibrator to test." She held up a smaller device with two control buttons and a flywheel. "Complete with a Bluetooth remote control. And the best thing is that it's whisper-quiet.

"Here," she said, handing me the flexible device. "See for yourself."

She tapped one of the buttons on the remote and the thick side of the contraption began buzzing softly in my hand.

"Okay," I nodded, looking around me to see if any other restaurant patrons were distracted by the gentle hum of the object. "It's *quiet* enough, but which end goes inside?"

"The bulbous end is a natural G-spot stimulator. You place the flatter end against your clit, then pull the thing up tight against your vulva to keep it snugly in place."

I suddenly became mindful of the wetness permeating my panties as I imagined the device vibrating inside me, surrounded by a bunch of oblivious bystanders.

"Can I give it a try here, like we did last time?" I grinned.

"No way," Hannah said, pulling the toy out of my hands. "There'll be no trial runs for this or any future tests. You'll just have to wait until we get to the church."

"And where will *you* be sitting while this is all going down?" I said.

"Right next to you, of course. I'll want a front-row seat to watch all the action."

<hr>

On Sunday morning, Hannah picked me up and drove me the two miles to our local church. The entire time I squirmed in my seat trying to imagine what it would be like having a vibrator buzzing inside me in the quiet chapel. When we got to the church parking lot, she pulled into a sheltered space then plucked the blue vibrator out of her purse and handed it to me, resting her arm on the seat cushion expectantly.

"*What?*" I said. "You don't trust me to put it in privately?"

"Not really," she smirked. "For all I know, you might pull on some adult diapers under your skirt to hide any unintended releases. Here," she said, handing me a plastic vial. "I brought some lube to make it go in easier."

"I don't need any," I said, pulling the vibrator out of her hands and placing it under my skirt. "I'm already plenty worked up thinking about this scenario."

"I hope you're wearing panties under that skirt," Hannah said, watching me shift my weight as I placed the device against my vulva. "We wouldn't want it popping out at an inopportune moment."

"I'll just have to leave that up to your imagination," I sneered, lifting my skirt halfway up my thigh. "Unless you need to inspect the goods to make sure I'm not cheating."

"I trust you," Hannah smiled, opening her car door. "Something tells me you're looking forward to this just as much as I am."

As we approached the entrance to the church, I noticed a familiar figure standing at the top of the steps greeting the incoming parishioners, and he made eye contact with me when Hannah and I approached the landing.

"Jade!" Father Fife said, holding out his hands to me. "I haven't seen you in such a long time. It's so good to have you join us again."

"I'm sorry, Father," I said, placing my sweaty hand between his. "I've been a little distracted lately..."

"Life has a habit of getting in the way of the important things," he said. "We're just glad to have you whenever you can find time." He turned to Hannah, raising his eyebrows in curiosity. "And who's this lovely lady you've brought with you to attend our service today?"

"This is Hannah," I said, motioning toward my friend. "I thought I'd bring her along for moral support."

"Happy to have you, Hannah," Father Fife said, clasping Hannah's hands warmly. "The Lord knows we all need moral support wherever we can find it."

Hannah nodded politely, then the two of us walked through the entrance doors where I dipped my hand into the bowl of holy water and crossed my chest before continuing on toward the front of the chapel.

"*Jesus,*" Hannah whispered, peering around the imposing shrine. "Is it just me, or did that feel a little creepy? All that talk about *having* us and that prolonged hand-holding. Hasn't he been paying any attention to the me-too movement?"

"I'm not sure any of that applies to men of the *cloth,*" I chuckled. "But you better be careful about using the Lord's name like that around here. If anybody overhears you, you're liable to be burned at the stake."

The two of us stepped lively down the main aisle and finding a free spot in the front row, we took our seats flanked by two elderly couples. It was hard to imagine how Hannah would be able to use the remote-control device sandwiched so closely between other parishioners, and I crossed my legs, thankful for the brief respite. When everyone had filed into the chapel and the bell signaled the start of the service, a hush fell over the chamber and we all stood up as Father Fife walked onto the pulpit in his flowing robes.

"In the name of the Father, and of the Son, and of the Holy Spirit," he intoned solemnly.

"Amen," the congregation murmured in unison.

"The Lord be with you," he said.

"And with your spirit," the couples beside me retorted.

What the hell have I gotten myself into? I thought, feeling the flexible vibrator pressing against the inside of my closed legs. I didn't consider myself a terribly religious person, but being in this holy place surrounded by all the familiar rituals brought back all the old memories from my parents about the consequences of sinful behavior. *Surely getting secretly stimulated by a sex toy in the house of God will send me straight to hell.*

This was the point in the church service where everybody was supposed to take a moment to make a penitential act. While I listened to the other parishioners around me making their supplications, my knees began shaking as I made my own silent prayer for forgiveness.

"May Almighty God have mercy on us all," the priest said. "Forgive us our sins, and bring us to everlasting life."

"Amen," I joined in the congregation's response.

"Let us pray," Father Fife said, bowing his head.

As we closed our eyes and he began his opening prayer, Hannah nudged me with her knee and my mind raced with images of the pastor scornfully looking down at us while we played our blasphemous game. I peered up as he flapped his Bible closed, and caught him glancing in my direction.

"Through our Lord Jesus Christ, your Son," he said. "Who lives and reigns with you in the unity of the Holy Spirit, one God forever and ever."

"Amen," I said aloud, hoping he'd see me behaving like a good Catholic girl and turn his attention elsewhere.

He motioned for everyone to sit down and I was glad to get off my shaky feet onto the relative safety of the wooden pew.

"Good morning, ladies and gentlemen," he began his homily. "Today, I would like to talk with you about *morality*. Specifically, about the decaying state of society's morals in today's world. All around us we are surrounded by prurient symbols of modern decadence. First it was in the form of the printed word, then motion pictures, then the ubiquitous internet. It seems everywhere we turn, we are bombarded with profane and sacrilegious images."

I felt my heart pounding in my chest, like he was singling me out personally for my not-so-infrequent porn surfing.

"We seem to have forgotten," he railed, "the Lord's commandment that we shall not covet thy neighbor's wife. This admonition can be taken in its broadest context. Not only have many of you forsaken the sacred institution of marriage, but the egregious and widespread popularity of obscene *pornography* belies our unbridled lust and depravity. God slew Onan for spilling his seed, and so He will strike all others who practice self-abuse."

Hannah nudged her knee against mine, suddenly

reminding me why we were here. I was glad that she hadn't yet had the opportunity to take out her remote-control device, and I prayed that we'd be able to get through most of the service without her rudely interrupting it. I'd already begun to regret agreeing to this little venture, and I hoped that somehow we'd be able to bypass this first phase in her experiment.

"I'd like you to pick up your Bibles," Father Fife said, interrupting my thoughts. "And turn to Mark, Chapter 7, Verse 20."

Hannah and I reached down to pick up the bibles lying on the seat beside each of us, and we flipped to the indicated section.

"Read this passage with me, my friends," Father Fife instructed. "What comes *out* of a person is what defiles him," he enunciated, while the congregation quietly murmured along.

As I began to recite the passage along with him, I saw Hannah reach into her side pocket and place her closed hand between the book binding.

"For from within come evil thoughts," I continued reading as I peered out of the corner of my eye to see what she was up to.

"Sexual immorality, adultery, coveting, wickedness..." we read in unison.

Suddenly, I felt the interior end of the vibrator begin to tremble inside me and I stuttered, trying to finish the passage.

"Deceit...sensuality...envy..." I stammered, trying to catch my breath as I followed along. Hearing my labored recital, Hannah turned her head in my direction, acknowledging my silent suffering. She knew exactly what I was feeling and how difficult it was for me to remain composed as I read the script.

"All these evil things...come from *within*," I gulped as I began to feel the pleasure spread across my pelvic region. "And they defile a person."

"Consider these words carefully," the priest said, surveying my hunched-over posture. "For the Lord does not abide salacious thoughts and behavior. If you want passage into His Kingdom, you must be as pure and righteous as He."

He paused for a moment to let the message sink in, then he motioned with his two hands for us to be seated. I was grateful for the rest, and I froze upright in my chair trying to ignore the movement of the possessed instrument inside me.

"Let us consider for a moment *another* one of God's ten commandments," Father Fife continued. "Thou shall not commit *adultery*. The Lord made Eve from the flesh of Adam, and in so doing signified that forever more man shall be united to his wife as one..."

As Father Fife ramped up the intensity of his gayphobic critique, so did Hannah, furtively adjusting the flywheel on the remote-control device nestled under her palm in her lap. As she slowly increased the speed of the vibrations emanating inside my pussy, I squirmed on the bench, trying to restrain my rising passion.

"By rejecting the sanctity of marriage," Father Fife continued, glancing distractedly in my direction, "you have all *sinned*. In the book of Deuteronomy, we saw that God ordered adulterers be stoned to death. For your indiscriminate behavior, so shall the Lord indiscriminately smite thee."

Jesus, I thought. If that's what awaits a sinner for

cheating on their spouse, I wonder what happens to someone who self-abuses herself while sitting for Sunday Service in a house of God. *Surely I'll burn in hell for this act of sacrilege.*

Just when I thought I was beginning to get control over the delicious sensations stimulating my insides, Father Fife instructed us to stand once again and recite another passage from the Bible.

"Please stand now and read Peter 1:16 with me," he said.

Everyone stood and dutifully flipped to the relevant section of the scriptures. This time it was even harder for me to stand motionless, as my knees fluttered unsteadily from the pleasurable sensations radiating inside me.

"It is written..." I tried to read along. "That you shall be holy, for I am holy."

I saw Hannah's hands moving once again inside her prayer book, and suddenly I felt the *other* end of the U-shaped vibrator buzzing against my clit.

"And now Galatians 5:16," Father Fife instructed, barely giving me a chance to recover.

I flipped to the new citation and gasped for breath as my legs wobbled beneath me.

"But I say," I panted unsteadily. "Walk by the Spirit, and you will not gratify the desires of the flesh."

"So it is written," Father Fife said, closing his Bible. "Be righteous as the Lord, and you shall join him in Heaven for everlasting days. And now," he said, magnifying my torture. "I would like us to sing together one of my favorite hymns celebrating His blessing, *Amazing Grace*. Please pick up your hymn books and turn to page forty-three."

"Amazing grace, how sweet the sound," the priest began to sing as the entire congregation joined him in harmony.

"That saved a wretch like me," I sang along, trying to

ignore the message that seemed targeted directly at me. As I tried to hold the melody, Hannah cupped the remote-control device in her hand and turned the flywheel to its maximum setting.

"I once was lost, but now am found," I hyperventilated, pressing my legs together as hard as I could to stifle the rising passion that threatened to overtake me.

"Was blind, but now I see," I squealed, singing the last word decidedly off-pitch as Father Fife turned to see my entire body shaking as I belted the famous hymn.

By the time I'd finished the song, I'd somehow managed to keep it together and fight off the cresting passion that had threatened to put me over the edge. When we finally sat back down, Hannah mercifully turned the vibrator off, and I spread my hands over my ruffled skirt to signal that I'd managed to keep myself composed.

When the service was over and we walked up the aisle behind the rest of the assembly to exit the church, I couldn't wait to get out of the building to wash myself off, figuratively and literally. I was glad that we were at the back of the crowd so nobody could see the back of my skirt. I wasn't sure if my leaking pussy had left a stain, but I sure as hell didn't want one of the parishioners pointing it out. When we finally exited the entrance doors, Father Fife turned to the two of us and smiled.

"I noticed you seemed a little more passionate than usual reciting today's passages, Jade" he said to me.

"Yes, Father," I said, shaking his hand unsteadily. "I felt truly embodied by the spirit."

"And *you*, Hannah," he nodded. "Did you enjoy today's service also?"

"Oh yes," she said. "It was the most moving sermon I've attended in a long time."

"I hope you'll both come again," Father Fife said to the two of us.

"I'm sure we *will*, Father," Hannah smiled as we continued down the steps.

Like the second we get back home, I thought to myself, dying to tear off my clothes and squirt all over Hannah's face while she ate out my still-dripping pussy.

READ MORE...

ABOUT THE AUTHOR

If you would like to receive notification of new book(s) in Jade's Erotic Adventures, follow me at http://bookbub.com/authors/victoria-rush.

If you have a moment, please post a brief review on my Amazon book page at viewbook.at/firstlady . Even just a couple of sentences will help other readers find and enjoy this book as much as you hopefully did.

Follow, share, like, and comment at:

www.facebook.com/authorvictoriarush
www.pinterest.com/authorvictoriarush
www.twitter.com/authorvictoriarush
authorvictoriarush@outlook.com

Hope to see you again soon!